Something Special

Mr Tumble's Annual 2014

Contents

EGMONT

We bring stories to life

First published in Great Britain in 2013 by Egmont UK Limited,
The Yellow Building, 1 Nicholas Road, London W11 4AN

Written by Gemma Barder, Jude Exley, Laura Green and Jane Riordan.
Designed by Martin Aggett
Nursery Song illustrations by Richard Watson

SOMETHING SPECIAL™ Copyright © BBC 2004

ISBN 978 1 4052 6852 3
55956/1
Printed in Italy

Hello, Mr Tumble!

Let's all wave to Mr Tumble!

Take your hand.
Give it a go.
Move it around
And say, hello!

The Hello Song

Sing along with Mr Tumble!

Hello, hello,
How are you?
Hello, hello, it's good to see you.

I say hello,
To you and all your friends.
I say hello,
Let's meet them together,
Let's play together,
Let's have fun with friends!
We're all friends!

4

5

Lord Tumble is going to watch the game of football.

He wants the blue team to win.

6

Aunt Polly wants the red team to win.

7

At the football game
Lord Tumble waves a
blue banner.

8

Aunt Polly shakes her
red pom poms.

9

Mr Tumble scores a goal for
the blue team.

10

Grandad Tumble
is worried.

11

He doesn't think he is as good at football as Mr Tumble.

12

Aunt Polly sings a red team song, then Grandad Tumble scores a goal, too!

13

Well done everybody!

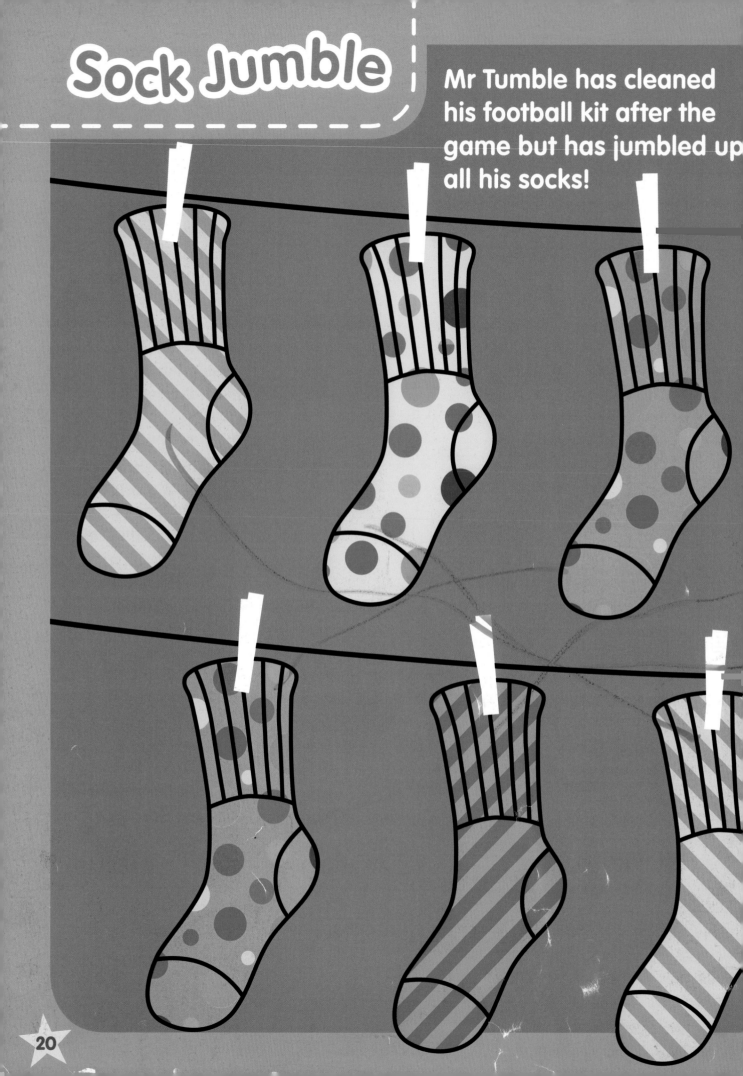

Can you help him match his socks? Draw a line between the socks that look the same.

Meet Grandad Tumble

Grandad Tumble has fallen asleep. Zzzzzzzz! Let's wake him up.

hat

round glasses

Shout Grandad as loud as you can.
Grandad!

spotty scarf

warm coat

purple patch

Can you colour Grandad Tumble's red scarf?

Chilly Colour Fun

Playing with ice is fun! Make ice even more fun by making some brightly-coloured ice cubes.

You will need:

An ice cube tray
Water
Food colour
Glasses or clear cups

All you need to do is:

1 Fill an ice cube tray with water.
2 Add a drop of food colouring to each compartment. You can make lots of different colours.
3 Put them in the freezer until they are solid.
4 Fill glasses with water and watch what happens as you drop a coloured ice cube in each glass.
5 You can try putting two ice cubes of different colours in the glass. Look to see what happens when the colours mix!

Blue

Green

Pink

Purple

Yellow

Did you have fun
with the cold ice
cubes Mr Tumble?
Brrr...

29

Crazy Colour Dance

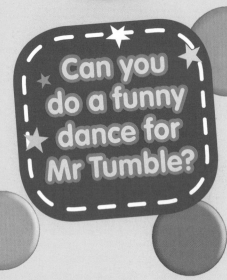

Can you do a funny dance for Mr Tumble?

Mr Tumble and Grandad Tumble are dancing! They're funny! Can you colour them in?

The Tumble Bird

1 Grandad Tumble is getting his camera ready.

2 He wants to take a photograph of a very special bird.

3 The Tumble Bird!

4 Grandad Tumble puts bird seed on the bird table.

5 He waits for the Tumble Bird to come. He waits a long time.

6 Look, the Tumble Bird has come to eat the bird seed.

... frightens the bird away.

7 Grandad Tumble knocks over his camera and ...

8

So Grandad Tumble has to wait for the Tumble Bird to come back again.

9

Mr Tumble arrives at Grandad Tumble's shed.

10

He's got a special surprise for Grandad Tumble.

11

He's going to play the trumpet. The trumpet scares the Tumble Bird away again.

2 Mr Tumble feels sad, but then he has a great idea!

13 Grandad Tumble sees a big bird eating seed from his table. Is it the Tumble Bird?

4 No! It's Mr Tumble dressed up in feathers. What fun!

Feathered Friends

Look at these funny birds.

How many yellow birds can you count?

How many red birds can you count?

Which bird do you think is the youngest?

Point to the bird who is flying.

Now colour in these birds in your favourite colours.

Spot the Difference

1

These two pictures of Mr Tumble look the same, but there are 5 differences in picture 2. Can you find them all?

Answers: Aunt Polly has appeared, there is a picture on the wall, the fireplace has changed from red to blue, a bucket of balls has appeared and the chair has changed from orange to green.

Meet Lord Tumble

Lord Tumble always looks very smart. He loves having lots of fun too. Every day is a party for Lord Tumble!

top hat

monocle to help him see

pink scarf

tail coat

Can you colour in Lord Tumble's black hat?

Meet Fisherman Tumble

Fisherman Tumble loves to sail his little boat out to sea. He catches lots of fish and sings sea songs too!

Captain's hat

hairy beard!

orange shirt

fishing rod

Colour the fish on the end of Fisherman Tumble's line!

Incy Wincy Spider

Incy wincy spider

climbed up the water spout.

Can you join in this song about a little spider?

Down came the rain

and washed the spider out.

Out came the sunshine

and dried up all the rain,

So incy wincy spider

climbed up the spout again!

43

Spotty Dotty Biscuits

Baker Tumble has made a tray of delicious spotty biscuits. You can make some too!

Ingredients:

300g self-raising flour

30g cocoa powder

250g margarine or soft butter

125g caster sugar

1 pack of dotty chocolate sweets

You will need:

A sieve

A wooden spoon

2 mixing bowls

Baking trays

All you need to do is:

1. Preheat the oven to 160ºC, Gas Mark 3.

2. Sieve the flour and cocoa into a bowl.

3. In another bowl, cream the margarine and sugar together. Then stir the flour and cocoa into the mixture to make a dough.

4. Roll the dough into small balls then put them on the baking trays leaving lots of space between them.

5. Flatten each biscuit with the back of a spoon, then decorate with spotty sweets and place in the oven.

6. Bake for about 10 minutes until the biscuits feel firm on top. Then put them on a rack to cool.

Always ask an adult to help you when using a hot oven.

Thank you Baker Tumble, your spotty biscuits are delicious!

Spot-to-Spot Fishing

Fisherman Tumble is ready to go fishing, but he'll need a river first. Follow the spots with your coloured crayons to finish the picture for him.

Now draw a fish on the end of Fisherman Tumble's fishing line.

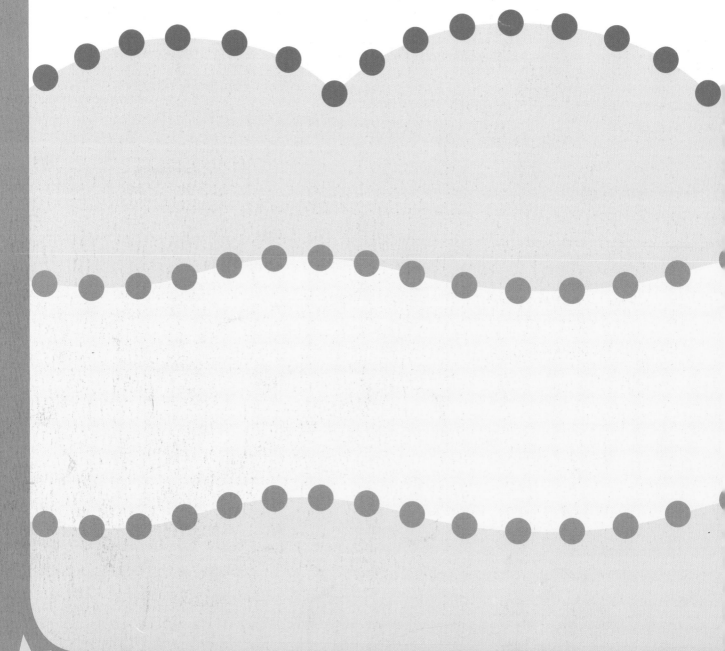

Mr Tumble's Oldest Friend

Mr Tumble is tidying his room. He's getting ready for a special party.

It's a party for Mr Tumble's oldest friend.

I wonder who Mr Tumble's oldest friend is. Do you know?

4

5

Aunt Polly and Lord Tumble are going to sing a song for Mr Tumble's friend.

It is a surprise.

6

They come to Mr Tumble's house to practise their song.

7 Aunt Polly sings and Lord Tumble plays the piano.

8 They all turn out the lights and wait for Mr Tumble's oldest friend to come.

9 Surprise ... it's Grandad Tumble!

10 Of course Grandad Tumble is Mr Tumble's oldest friend

11

12

Aunt Polly and Lord Tumble play their song.

Grandad Tumble is very happy.

Memory Game

Can you remember what happened in the story?

① Who played the piano?

(a)

(b)

(c)

② Who sang a song?

(a)

(b)

(c)

③ Who was Mr Tumble's oldest friend?

(a)

(b)

(c)

Everybody Count!

There are five presents for Grandad Tumble hiding in the picture. Can you find them all?

I wonder what is inside each present ...

Meet Chef Tumble

chef's hat

Look at Chef Tumble. He is so dirty! He makes a mess when he cooks so you'd better watch out!

curly moustache!

grubby coat!

Colour ★ the wibbly wobbly jelly ★ green!

checked trousers

red shoes

What do you like to eat?

Meet Cliff Tumble

orange sunglasses

Cliff Tumble is a pop star! He sings songs to Aunt Polly. He likes to blow her kisses too. MWAH!

blue tie

Colour Cliff Tumble's microphone.

flowery shirt

sparkly coat

What do you like to sing?

Where We Live

Mr Tumble lives in a house with a yellow, spotty door! Can you draw a door and some windows on this house?

Twinkle, twinkle,
little star,
How I wonder
what you are.

Make a Noise!

Make a noise with Mr Tumble.

Mr Tumble is funny and today Mr Tumble is making music. You can too when you make a maraca just like Mr Tumble's.

You will need:

- Water bottle
- Masking tape
- Paint
- Paintbrush
- Marker pens
- Paper for funnel
- 2 handfuls of uncooked rice or pasta

All you need to do is:

1

Wrap an empty water bottle with masking tape. Don't cover the cap.

3

Decorate the bottle using paint or markers. Then leave it to dry.

60

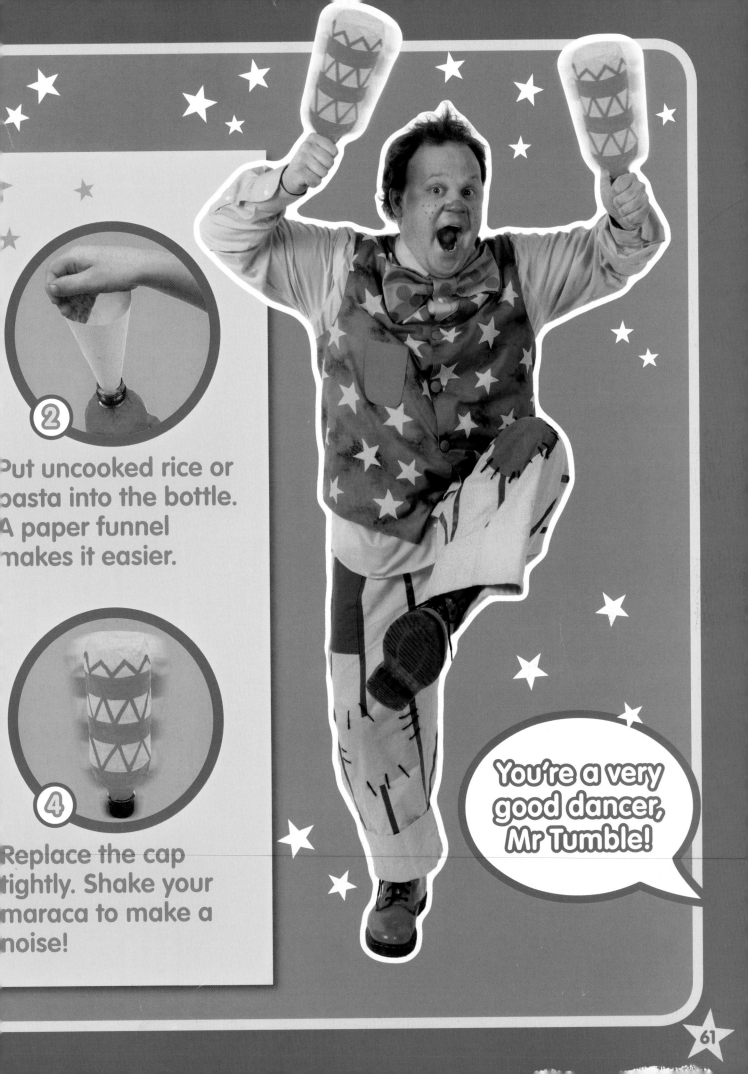

②

Put uncooked rice or pasta into the bottle. A paper funnel makes it easier.

④

Replace the cap tightly. Shake your maraca to make a noise!

You're a very good dancer, Mr Tumble!

Balloon Bonanza

Start →

Mr Tumble is going to a birthday party! But he's lost.

Use your finger to guide Mr Tumble through the maze to the party. Make sure you pass all of the party balloons along the way!

Finish →

63

Goodbye Song

Now it's time to say goodbye. Sing along with Mr Tumble!

Goodbye Colouring

Colour in Mr Tumble
like the little picture.

Then wave goodbye.

Goodbye!

Something Special Reader Survey 2014

You are funny Mr Tumble!

We'd love to know what you think about your Something Special Annual.

Ask a grown-up to help you fill in this form and post it to the address at the end by 28th February 2014, or you can fill in the survey online at: www.egmont.co.uk/somethingspecialsurvey2014

One lucky reader will win £150 of book tokens.
Five runners up will win a £25 book token each.

1. Who bought this annual?

☐ Me

☐ Parent/guardian

☐ Grandparent

☐ Other (please specify)

_____

2. Why did they buy it?

☐ Christmas present

☐ Birthday present

☐ I'm a collector

☐ Other (please specify)

_____

3. What are your favourite parts of the Annual?

	Really like	Like	Don't like
Stories	☐	☐	☐
Puzzles	☐	☐	☐
Colouring	☐	☐	☐
Meet the characters	☐	☐	☐
Songs and rhymes	☐	☐	☐
Things to make	☐	☐	☐

4. Do you think the stories are too long, too short or about right?

☐ Too long ☐ Too short ☐ About right

5. Do you think the activities are too hard, too easy or about right?

☐ Too hard ☐ Too easy ☐ About right

6. Apart from Mr Tumble, who are your favourite characters?

1. ....
2. ....
3. ....

7. Which other annuals do you like?

1. ....
2. ....
3. ....

8. What is your favourite …

1. … app or website? ....

2. … console game? ....

3. … magazine? ....

4. … book? ....

9. What are your favourite TV programmes?

1. ....
2. ....
3. ....

10. Would you like to get the Something Special Annual again next year?

☐ Yes   ☐ No

Why? ....

....

Name: Age: .... Boy ☐   Girl ☐

Signature: ....

Email address: ....

Daytime telephone number: ....

☐ Please send me the Egmont Monthly Catch-Up Newsletter.

Please cut out and post to:

**Something Special Annual Reader Survey, Egmont UK Limited,
The Yellow Building, 1 Nicholas Road, London, W11 4AN** .... **Good luck!**